This igloo book belongs to:

....

Published in 2013
by Igloo Books Ltd
Cottage Farm
Sywell
NN6 0BJ
www.igloobooks.com

OCE001 0813
2 4 6 8 10 9 7 5 3
ISBN: 978-1-78197-009-6

Written by Jenny Woods
Illustrated by Anna Jones

Printed and manufactured in China

Princess

Stories

iglóobooks

Contents

One Sweet Treat

Princess Katie was watching Cook bake a batch of delicious cupcakes in the palace kitchen and she couldn't help licking her lips. "Please can I have one?" Katie begged, but Cook shook her head. "The queen is keeping these cakes for something special," said Cook.

The princess stomped her feet, feeling cross. "It's not fair," she moaned. "I only wanted one sweet treat."

When the cook had gone out, Katie crept up to the table and took one of the cupcakes. It was so yummy that she ate another and another, until they were all gone.

...le while later, ...k and found Katie holding her tummy and groaning loudly. "W... ...re all the cakes?" she cried. "They were for the queen's roy... ...party this afternoon." "I ate them all," moaned Katie, "and ... ...eel sick."

FLOUR

"You will have to help me make some more," said Cook, firmly.
She gave Katie a flowery apron to put on. The princess didn't feel
like cooking at all, but she helped mix and bake a big batch of
lovely, new cupcakes, just in time for the party.

When the cakes were ready, Katie carefully topped each one with a swirl of pretty icing. Then, she decorated them with little sugar flowers and sprinkles. The new cupcakes looked amazing and Katie couldn't wait to show them to the queen.

Everyone at the party thought the cupcakes were delicious.
"You can have one as a treat if you like," said the queen to Katie.
Katie looked at Cook and smiled. "No thanks," she said. "I think
I've had enough of cupcakes for one day!"

Beatrice the Ballerina

"I want to be a ballerina," announced Princess Beatrice one day, twirling daintily across the palace floor. She pointed her toes and leapt in the air, but the queen was too busy counting her crowns to watch. "18, 19, 20... sorry, I can't stop now," she said. "Go and tell your father."

So, Beatrice danced off to find the king, who was listening to the royal musicians. "Look at me, I can do a pirouette," she said.
"I can't look now," the king shouted over the loud music. "Show me later."
"Hmph!" said the princess. "Everyone's too busy to watch me dance."

13

That night, Princess Beatrice had a brilliant idea. She crept out of bed and tiptoed quietly down the stairs. In the music room, the royal musicians were packing away their instruments. "Please could you help me choose some music," asked Beatrice. "I want to put on a secret ballet show and I need your help."

The following night, Beatrice visited the royal dressmaker.
She picked out some shiny satin, pretty frills and lots and lots of
sparkly sequins. The dressmaker measured and cut and stitched
and sewed. By the end of the night, she had helped Beatrice to
make a beautiful ballet dress.

Next, Beatrice asked the royal artist to paint her some scenery. Then, she trotted down to the kitchen to see if the cook could whizz up lots of yummy treats. Finally, she set to work making invitations. Soon, everything was ready for the secret show.

The next day, the king and queen gathered in the royal hall.
They gasped in amazement when the curtain went up and Princess
Beatrice whirled and twirled across the stage. "What a wonderful
performance," said the king, clapping as hard as he could.
Beatrice smiled and gave a curtsy. Being a ballerina was brilliant!

The Perfect Pet

Princess Lily longed to have a pet, but no matter how much she begged the king and queen, they always said no. So, one day, Lily decided to buy a pet for herself. While the queen was busy chatting, she went into the local pet shop to look at the animals.

There were all sorts of adorable animals, but the one that Lily
liked the most was the cutest of all. It was a baby dragon with
shiny, purple scales and little, pink wings. "I'm sure you won't be
any trouble at all," said Lily, holding the dragon in her hands.

When Lily got home, the dragon knocked over a suit of armour and scratched the king's throne with its sharp claws. The king was furious until the baby dragon curled up on his lap. "It is rather cute," he admitted. Then, the dragon burped and set fire to his beard.

That afternoon, the queen found the baby dragon chewing on her best shoes. When she told it off, the dragon flapped its little wings and flew unsteadily round the room, bumping into ornaments and pictures. "That pet has got to go," the king and queen told Princess Lily.

So, Lily scooped the baby dragon into her backpack and set off to the pet shop to take it back. "I'm sure they will find you a lovely, new home," she sighed, giving the dragon a last kiss on its scaly, little nose. Then, she made her way home, feeling sad.

When Princess Lily arrived at the palace, the king and queen were waiting for her in the garden. "We have decided that you can have a pet after all," said the queen, "but only if it's a rabbit," she added. Lily was very happy. The dragon had been fun, but a cute, baby bunny was even better and much less trouble!

Princess Harriet's Hiccups

Princess Harriet could not stop hiccupping. She hiccupped while she ate her breakfast and spilt cereal everywhere. She hiccupped while she drank her orange juice and knocked it all over the royal butler. She even scared the palace cat away with a very loud, "HICCUP!"

"Please help me get rid of my hiccups," she begged the butler, who was wiping orange juice off his face.

"Try holding your breath and hopping on one leg," he suggested.

Harriet wobbled round the room and her face went redder and redder until she let out one enormous, "HICCUP!"

"Well, that didn't work," said Harriet and she set off to see the king, who was watching TV in the palace living room.

"Put your socks on your hands and do a handstand," he said, when she asked him what to do. "It always works for me."

Harriet did as her father said, but it made her hiccups worse.

Next, Harriet went to find the queen, who was reading a book in the library. "Getting rid of hiccups is easy," said the queen. "Just balance a book on your head and walk backwards."

Harriet picked up the nearest book and took a step back, but she almost trod on the cat's tail as she gave a loud, "HICCUP!"

"Perhaps some fresh air will help," thought Harriet, stepping out into the garden with a, "Hiccup!"

The royal gardener heard Harriet's hiccups and had an idea. "Puff out your cheeks and jump like a monkey," he said.

So, Harriet puffed out her cheeks and jumped around.

Suddenly, Harriet spotted her reflection in one of the palace windows. "I look so silly," she said and burst out laughing.

Princess Harriet laughed and laughed. When she finally stopped, the hiccups had gone. At last, she had found out how to cure hiccups. "Next time, I will just remember to laugh!" she said.

Bella's Ball Gown

It was the day of the palace ball and the queen wanted Princess Bella to wear a pretty dress. "I don't want to go to the ball," complained Bella. "I'd rather ride my bike instead." "You'll enjoy it, I promise," said the queen. Then, she gave the dress to Bella and left her to put it on.

"This dress is boring, but I know how to make it look much better,"
thought Bella. She grabbed the gown and hurried off to the garden.
"Please may I have some flowers?" she asked the gardener politely.
"Of course," he said, picking out the prettiest ones for her.

Next, Bella visited the royal jeweller, who was busy counting rubies. "Excuse me," said Bella, "have you got any spare jewels I could borrow?"

The jeweller found some super, sparkly gems that had fallen off an old crown. "Perfect," said Bella. "Now there's one last person to visit."

In the palace sewing room, the royal dressmaker helped Bella stitch all the flowers and jewels onto her dress.

When they had finished, Bella dashed off to get ready. "I don't want to be late for the ball," she thought.

33

Bella burst into the ballroom just as the band started playing. Everybody stopped dancing to look at her and her amazing dress. The gems sparkled under the lights and the flowers smelled so pretty. Bella had the best dress at the ball.

"Now you look like a real princess," smiled the queen.
Bella grinned, lifted up the hem of her dress and trotted onto
the dance floor. The ball wasn't so bad after all and no one had
even noticed that she was still wearing her trainers!

Princess Pippa's Present

Princess Pippa was getting ready for her best friend's birthday party. She put on her party dress and brushed her hair until it shone. Then, she picked up the bunch of flowers she had bought as a present for Princess Rosie and got a nasty surprise.

A slimy slug had slithered over the leaves and munched on all the pretty petals. "Yuck!" cried Pippa. "I can't give these flowers to Rosie now." Luckily, Pippa had another present for her friend. She grabbed the wrapping paper and dashed to the kitchen to find it.

"Do you want a chocolate?" said the king, offering Pippa a strawberry fudge cream, as she walked into the room.
"Oh, no," howled Pippa. "I bought those especially for Rosie."
"Mmm," said the king, eating the last one, "they are yummy!"

"I could still give Rosie that necklace I bought the other day,"
thought Pippa, rushing off to find it. She ran past her little sister,
Poppy, and spotted the necklace on one of Poppy's dolls. "Give that
back!" she cried, grabbing it. Snap! The string broke and sparkling
beads flew all over the room.

"I can't go to the party without a present for Rosie!" cried Pippa. "Don't worry, we'll make something," said Poppy, kindly. So, the two sisters got out their craft box and set to work. Pippa stuck on shiny sequins while Poppy sprinkled lots and lots of sparkly glitter.

When Princess Pippa arrived at the birthday party, Princess Rosie couldn't wait to open her present. She eagerly tore off all the wrapping paper and then gave a huge smile. "What a lovely birthday crown," she said, placing it carefully on her head. "Thank you, Pippa. It really is the perfect present!"

The Palace Pet Show

Princess Amelia was very excited. It was the day of the palace pet show and she had spent all morning trying to make her pony, Popcorn, look perfect. She combed his mane, covered his new saddle in sparkly glitter and made him a special headband of jewels and fluffy feathers.

Amelia thought Popcorn looked wonderful, but he wasn't happy at all. He didn't like being dressed up. He was much happier when he could just be himself. One of the feathers tickled Popcorn's nose and he gave a giant sneeze, "ACHOO!"

Amelia could see how unhappy Popcorn was. She took off the scratchy saddle and combed out his mane and tail. Then, she threw away the tickly headband and they set off for the show. "We may not win any prizes," said Amelia, stroking her pony's silky mane," but at least you'll be happy and that's what really matters!"

There were pets from all over the kingdom at the show.
There were big ones, small ones, furry ones and fluffy ones.
There was a pig wearing clothes, a rabbit in a hat and even a chicken
wearing a crown. The problem was, all of them looked unhappy.

One-by-one the pets paraded past the judges' table. Popcorn and Amelia waited for their turn, standing next to a shimmery peacock and a pink poodle with a silly hairstyle. "Popcorn looks so plain, we'll never win," thought Amelia.

When it was their turn, Amelia felt nervous, but Popcorn held his head up high and trotted across the ring. He whinnied and tossed his mane, neighing happily at the judges. Suddenly, Amelia realised that Popcorn looked good, no matter what he was wearing!

The judges were very impressed with Popcorn. "This pony wins first place," they said. "He's the happiest pet we've seen all day."

So, Amelia was given a huge trophy and Popcorn got a rosette. Amelia was so proud of Popcorn, she was the happiest girl at the pet show that day, too.